Caillou

Merry Christmas!

Text: Johanne Mercier • Illustrations: Pierre Brignaud • Coloration: Marcel Depratto

chouette

Everyone in Caillou's family
is getting ready to celebrate
Christmas! Grandma and
Grandpa are visiting.
So is Aunt Poppy, who
has brought along Balthazar,
her big cat.

Grandma and Mommy
are baking cookies in the shape
of stars. Balthazar sits
in a corner of the kitchen,
hoping for a treat.

In the living room,
Aunt Poppy and Grandpa
are singing Christmas songs.
Caillou would like to sing
along, but he's having
trouble sitting still.
"Is tonight Christmas Eve?"
Caillou asks Daddy
for the hundredth time.

Before going to bed,
Caillou puts three cookies
and a glass of milk on a
table in the living room.
"These are for Santa Claus,"
Caillou whispers to Rosie.

Caillou is having a lot of
trouble falling asleep.
He has been waiting so long
for this night to arrive! Finally,
he sleeps, dreaming of all
the presents Santa will bring him.

In the middle of the night,
a strange noise wakes Caillou up.
It's coming from the living room.
Caillou is sure it's Santa!

Caillou gets out of bed and
tiptoes downstairs, being careful
not to make any noise.
He especially doesn't want
to wake up Rosie.

Caillou's heart is beating
very fast. The glass of milk
is almost empty and
the cookies are gone!
"Santa must be nearby."
Caillou thinks.

Caillou is very excited, but walks
cautiously through the living room.
Suddenly, he sees two bright
green eyes staring at him!

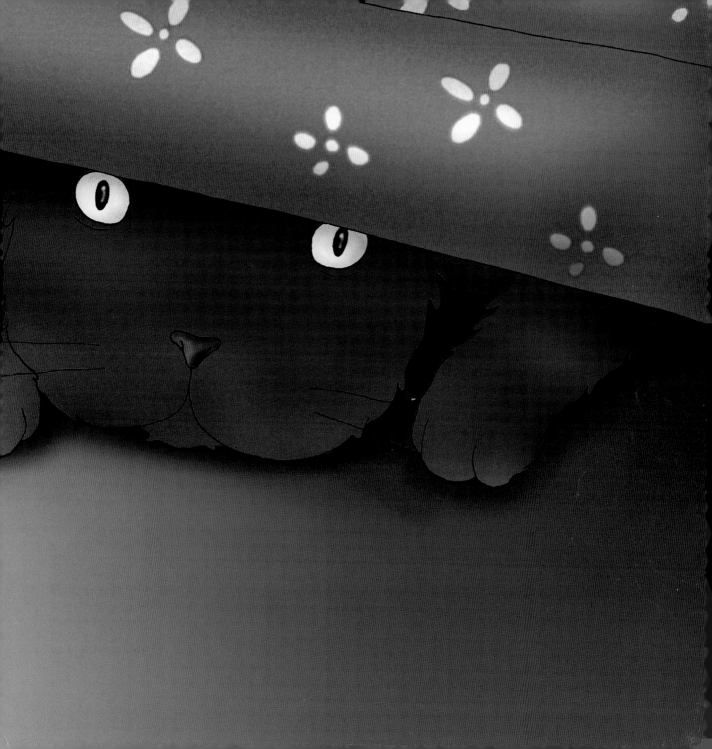

"Balthazar! What are you doing there?!" Caillou scolds Aunt Poppy's cat. Balthazar is pushing the cookies around on the floor. His whiskers are still white from drinking the milk. Caillou goes back to bed, a little disappointed. He wishes he had seen Santa. Balthazar follows him, purring happily.

Caillou is the first one awake
on Christmas morning.
He runs downstairs.
"Rosie! Rosie, come see!" Caillou
shouts when he sees all the
presents Santa has left under the
Christmas tree. There is something
for everyone. Even for that
naughty cat, Balthazar!

Text: Johanne Mercier
Illustrations: Pierre Brignaud
Coloration: Marcel Depratto
Art Director: Monique Dupras

The PBS KIDS logo is a registered mark of PBS and is used with permission.

We acknowledge the financial support of the Government of Canada through the Canada Book Fund for our publishing activities.

Canadian Heritage   Patrimoine canadien

We acknowledge the support of the Ministry of Culture and Communications of Quebec and SODEC for the publication and promotion of this book.

SODEC
Québec

National Library of Canada cataloguing in publication data

Mercier, Johanne
Caillou: merry Christmas!
3rd ed.
(Confetti)
Translation of: Caillou : Joyeux Noël!.
For children aged 2 and up.

ISBN 978-2-89718-020-1

1. Christmas - Juvenile literature. 2. Gifts - Juvenile literature. I. Brignaud, Pierre. II. Title. III. Title: Merry Christmas!. IV. Series: Confetti (Montréal, Québec).

GT4985.5.M4713 2012   j394.2663   C2012-940525-6

Printed in Guangdong, China
10 9 8 7 6 5 4 3 2 1 CHO1840 MAY2012